Series 549

A Ladybird
Robin Hood Adventure

# The
# Silver Arrow

*A story by* MAX KESTER

*Illustrated by*
JOHN KENNEY

Publishers: Ladybird Books Ltd . Loughborough
© Ladybird Books Ltd (formerly Wills & Hepworth Ltd) 1954
*Printed in England*

# THE SILVER ARROW

The Sheriff of Nottingham sat in the great hall of Nottingham Castle biting his nails. He was very angry. His Steward stood before him, trembling all over. He had never seen his master in such a rage before.

" This outlaw Robin Hood must be captured! " he shouted, and banged the table so hard that the dishes sprang into the air.

" I've done my best," mumbled the frightened Steward, " but Robin Hood hides in the middle of Sherwood Forest, my Lord, and we can't find him anywhere."

The Sheriff sprang up and looked angrier than ever.

" He must be found. I will give a bag of gold to the first man who brings him into Nottingham Castle! "

Now the Sheriff of Nottingham was a hard, cruel man. Indeed, it was he who had seized Robin Hood's lands and home, and taken them for himself. What is more, ever since Robin Hood and his merry men (for he had a faithful band of followers) had gone into hiding, they had helped all the poor people who had got into trouble with the Sheriff. Robin was a great favourite with the townspeople and the villagers, and it was only the wicked proud Barons who hated and feared him.

And Robin, too, was the greatest archer in England. His bow, made out of the branch of a giant yew-tree, was taller than a man. Little Much, the Miller's son, who acted as the cook and general handy-man for the outlaws, couldn't even bend it ! The others stood around and laughed at him.

So, while the Sheriff was fuming and fretting in Nottingham Castle, Robin Hood was safe in Sherwood Forest. But outside the walls of Nottingham Castle, in the long meadow that led down to the River Trent there was great excitement.

It was Nottingham Goose Fair, when all the people from miles around brought their wares to sell, and enjoy the side-shows such as the wrestling, the jugglers, the pedlars and the ballad-singers who sang all the latest songs—many of them about Robin Hood. Everywhere gaily coloured stalls were being set up, and country folk were staggering in under loads of cheeses, pies, and rolls of cloth.

As he watched the preparations from the window of Nottingham Castle, the Sheriff had an idea. He sent for the Town Crier, the Mayor of Nottingham, and the Captain of his Men-at-Arms.

" I have an idea how we may capture this bold Robin Hood," he told them. " He thinks himself the greatest archer in England, so we will have a competition, with a prize. We will give a shining silver arrow, which shall be carried through the town on a crimson velvet cushion and you, Master Crier, will ring your bell, and cry aloud to all the people that he who hits the target three times shall bear the name of Champion Archer of England. That will bring Robin Hood out of hiding, and we shall be able to catch him without much difficulty.

They all thought that was a splendid idea. Then the Mayor of Nottingham said to the Sheriff, " But, my Lord, what if he comes in disguise, how shall we know him? "

" Pah," said the Sheriff. " We will make the mark to be shot at so difficult that nobody but Robin Hood can hit it! "

So it was decided, and the Town Crier, preceded by a boy bearing the silver arrow on the crimson cushion, went through the streets of the town telling everybody about the great competition.

Now it happened that jolly Friar Tuck, one of Robin's band, was in Nottingham, and after he had listened to the Town Crier, he girded up his robes, and ran for all he was worth to carry the news to Robin Hood.

Up in the highest branches of the huge oak tree in Sherwood Forest, which was the meeting place of the band of outlaws, Robin Hood himself, clad in his suit of Lincoln Green, which enabled him to hide among the bushes and trees without being seen, shaded his eyes with his hand as he looked out to see if any danger was approaching. Then suddenly the outlaws gathered below heard Robin give a loud laugh, and soon he came leaping down nimbly from the branches.

" What is it? " cried Little John, who, far from being little, was the biggest of them all. " What have you seen? "

" Friar Tuck is coming this way, running like a stag," he said.

" Oh, Robin, is he being chased by the Sheriff? " cried Much, the Miller's son.

" Not he," laughed Robin. " But he looks as if he has some news for us."

" Aha," said Little John, " perhaps he is going to tell us of a band of wicked Barons, with pack-horses laden with gold."

" Yes," said Will Scarlett, " and we can take the gold from them—because, of course, they will have stolen it from others —and give it to the poor folk round here who have hardly enough to eat."

" We shall see," said Robin Hood.

And they all began sharpening their swords, and seeing that their bows and arrows were in good order.

In a few minutes Friar Tuck ran up, panting, for he was very fat, and when Robin heard the news about the silver arrow he was determined to win it.

" You are going to do no such thing," cried Little John. " What, go into the net the Sheriff has spread for you? This is just a trap, because he knows you cannot resist showing your skill as an archer! "

But Robin had set his heart on winning the silver arrow.

" I shall go disguised, and call myself Robert of Locksley," he said. " And fear not, I shall come home safely, and bring the silver arrow with me."

The next morning, before the sun was above the tops of the oak trees, he dressed himself in an old leather jerkin with a hood to hide his face, and set off for Nottingham Goose Fair. He thought the other outlaws were still fast asleep on the mossy grass under the trees, but he was mistaken. Little John was not asleep, for when Robin was out of sight he sprang up and woke Will Scarlett and Alan-a-dale.

"Robin is headstrong and stubborn," he told them. "He has crept off to put his head in a noose. We will follow him, and if the proud Sheriff tries any tricks, we shall be there to give help."

They now belted on their swords, took their bows and arrows, and keeping out of sight of Robin, who was marching ahead singing merrily, they followed him to Nottingham.

The Sheriff of Nottingham was also awake as early as Robin, and called the Captain of his Men-at-Arms. Out they went to the long meadow, where a great striped canopy had been erected for the high officials who were going to watch the archery contest.

" Now, Captain," said the Sheriff, "place your Men-at-Arms, with their cross-bows and spears, round the ground. Tell them to hinder no man who wishes to come in. But, mark well, they must keep their eyes on me, and when I am about to give the silver arrow to the winner—who is sure to be Robin Hood—they must rush in and seize him, and bind him fast."

" I shall do all you say, my lord Sheriff," replied the Captain of the Men-at-Arms.

Soon the crowds were watching the serving men set up the targets for the archers. They set them up at one end of the meadow. Three targets, and a hundred paces away, the contestants began to gather to shoot for the prize.

" Marry! " cried one of them, " to hit the targets at that distance is too much to ask. They are too far by half ! "

Many of the others agreed, but they were very surprised when a man in a leather jerkin, with a hood over his face, spoke up suddenly.

" Too far? " he cried scornfully. " Nay, they are too near—and too large! This is what we should shoot at, to be worthy of the name of Champion Archer of England." And he brought out of his quiver three peeled willow wands, each about as long as an arrow, and no thicker than a man's thumb.

What a cry of derision went up! "Why," the contestants cried, "even Robin Hood himself couldn't hit those!"

"We shall see," said the hooded stranger, and after a lot of argument and discussion with the master of the contest, it was agreed that the distance should be reduced to fifty paces.

Then the shooting began. Some of the archers missed the wands completely. Some hit one of them, and one man, a bowman whose name was Diccon of Trent, managed to split two of the willow wands, but missed the third.

"Diccon's the winner!" cried the crowd, as they threw their caps in the air. But at that moment, quite un-noticed by any of the crowd, Little John and his two companions edged their way to the front of the spectators not far from the gilded chair on which the Sheriff was sitting.

" By my troth," muttered Little John, " our Robin has given himself a hard task. He will never better that shooting! "

But Robin, out in the middle of the field was walking *away* from the target! Yes, he was walking a full hundred paces away. Then he turned, and quicker than the eye could see, drew his mighty bow and loosed the first shaft. Quickly it sped to its mark and split the willow wand in twain!

A gasp of admiration went up from the crowd.

The second arrow did the same, and as Robin took aim on the third a hush fell over the assembly. No one breathed as he drew back the arrow. Twang! went the bow-string.

" A hit! a hit!" cried the onlookers, and they went mad with excitement.

Slowly the Sheriff raised his hand and beckoned. There was a gleam of excitement in his eye. He took the cushion with the silver arrow on it from an attendant. Robin Hood came forward, the hood well over his face, and bowed low.

" You are a fine marksman, fellow," said the Sheriff. " What is your name? "

" Robert of Locksley, my lord Sheriff."

" Then Robert of Locksley," there was a snarl in his voice, " you are the winner of the Silver Arrow! "

And as he spoke these words he stood up and raised the arrow high in his hand. On this signal the watching Men-at-Arms sprang forward. Before Little John, Will Scarlett and Alan-a-dale could move a hand, Robin Hood was surrounded by a ring of steel.

" So, Robert of Locksley," snarled the Sheriff, " you think I do not know you. But I know full well that you are the bold outlaw Robin Hood, my deadly enemy! " He waved his hand. " Take him away, and chain him up in the safest dungeon in the castle! "

" What can we do? " said Will Scarlett, as they saw their friend being dragged away, watched by a wondering crowd.

" Nothing," replied Alan-a-dale, sadly, " once a man is in Nottingham Castle he can never be rescued."

" Pooh! " cried Little John. " There is no castle in England strong enough to hold Robin Hood for long. I have a plan."

And with that the others had to be content.

Next morning, the soldiers on the draw-bridge at Nottingham Castle looked out to see two stalwart countrymen approaching the gate. On their shoulders was a pole, and on it was slung the carcase of a fine fat deer.

" Ho there ! " cried the leader of the two men. " We bring venison for my lord the Sheriff. We are to take it to the kitchens to be roasted."

The soldiers put their heads together, but they let down the drawbridge so that the men could come in. They seemed harmless- enough, and had no knives or swords.

" Which way to the kitchens? " cried the first man, who was none other than Little John.

" Down the stone steps," said the soldier, little suspecting that the second man

was Will Scarlett, and that both were the last people who should have been allowed into the Castle.

Down the steps they went, but instead of going into the great kitchen, where the cooks were boiling and roasting and baking, and from which delicious smells were being wafted, the two conspirators, still carrying the deer, went on and on, down more and more steps, till they reached a dark corner where the walls were green with moss and a torch burned fitfully along a gloomy passage. Then silently and quickly, the pole was lowered, and the deer dumped on to the ground. Swiftly, Little John turned it on its back, and undid a leather lacing which sewed up its stomach. Out of the inside he brought ropes, swords, bow and arrows, and a heavy crowbar ! It was only a deerskin stuffed with hay, leaving room for the things they required

to rescue Robin Hood, for that was what they were going to try to do !

" Now," whispered Little John, " we must try to find out which dungeon Robin is in."

" There may be a guard outside the door," murmured Will, softly. Cautiously the two conspirators peeped out of their hiding place along the corridor. It was empty ! Suddenly there came the clanking of feet from round the corner. The two drew back and flattened themselves against the wall, their swords ready in their hands. Down the steps came two guards in chain mail, one of them with a drawn sword, and the other with a wooden platter of bread and meat.

Will and Little John looked at one another. Food for one of the prisoners ! But which one ? Perhaps there were more than one.

The soldiers clattered past along the passage. Little John beckoned to his companion, and in a trice they were going softly along the passage on tip-toe behind the soldiers. On marched the soldiers, suspecting nothing. They turned a corner, where the shadows were even darker than before. Then came a great rattling of bolts, locks and chains as a door creaked open. They heard the voice of one of the soldiers.

" Now, bold outlaw," it said, " we bring you your dinner. The Sheriff would not have you go hungry to-day, for to-morrow . . . "

But what the soldier was going to say we shall never know, for at that moment Little John and Will Scarlett hurled them both bodily through the open door of the cell with such force that they had all the breath knocked out of them, and lay there stunned.

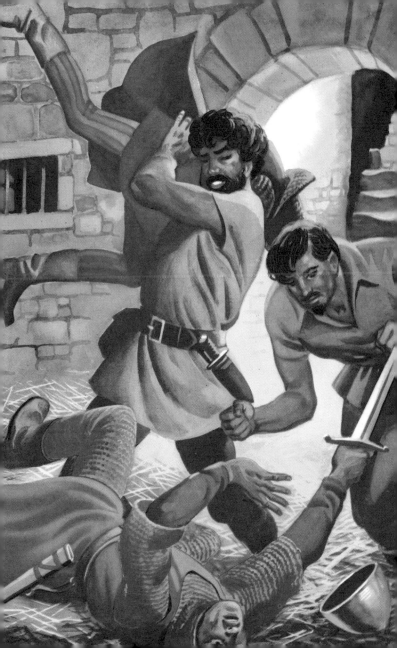

" Will ! John! " gasped Robin, in amazement.

" Shh! " panted John. " We must work fast."

First they darted back into the passage, their deerskin sandals making no noise, and brought the deerskin and all the other things into the cell. Then they shut the door. The next thing to do was to tie up and gag the two soldiers, first of all taking off their armour and surcoats which bore the colours of the Sheriff.

Robin was chained to the wall with an iron belt round his middle, and fastened with a strong padlock. Little John, that mighty man, put the end of the crowbar through the loop of the lock, and with a mighty wrench which nearly had Robin off his feet, he broke it open.

"All very well," said Robin, "but how do we get out of here? To fight our way out would be madness!"

For answer, Will Scarlett began pulling the hay out of the stuffed deerskin. Robin gave a chuckle. "A rare scheme, on my life," he said. But when the plan was explained to him, that he should get into the deerskin, while the others put on the soldiers chain-mail he looked grave.

"No, no," he said. "I have a better plan. It will seem more real."

And quickly he whispered to them what he proposed to do.

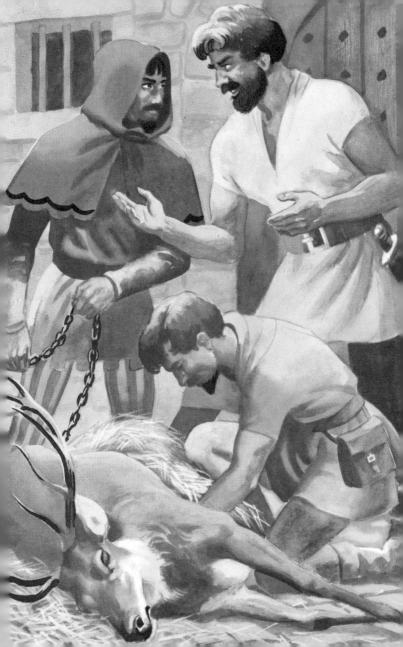

About ten minutes later the soldiers who were on guard at the drawbridge were surprised to see the same two countrymen, still carrying the deer slung on a pole, climbing up the steps from the kitchen and coming towards them.

" Why, fellows," said one of them, " could you not find the Sheriff's kitchen, then? "

" Ay," said the leader in a surly voice, " but Master Cook took one look at our fine stag here, and said it was bad meat, not fit for the Sheriff's table. He bid us take it back again to Sir Guy of Gisborne."

One of the soldiers prodded the stag with the butt of his spear. " In truth," he said, " it looks a sorry beast."

" Ah," said the second countryman, " but we're not going to carry it all that way, and get ourselves beaten by Sir Guy into the bargain, for sending his friend the Sheriff bad meat."

" What will you do, then? " asked the soldier, as he lowered the drawbridge for them.

" Why, we shall hurl it into the moat! "

And before the surprised soldiers' eyes, they tipped up the pole and sent the deer sliding into the water of the moat.

How the soldiers laughed. But they would not have laughed if they had seen how Robin Hood, the moment the deerskin touched the water, ripped it open with a knife and, swimming under the water, reached the bank, and climbed stealthily out among the reeds.

With a wave of the hand, Will Scarlett and Little John walked off down the road never once looking back.

That evening, in the great glade in Sherwood Forest there was a delicious smell of roast venison.

Robin Hood sat in the midst of his band of merry men with a tasty morsel on the end of his knife.

" By my faith! " said he, " I do not think there is a man in England who has such good comrades as I have." And he pointed to Will and John, who were munching away. " I was saved by the skin of my teeth! "

" Nay," said fat Friar Tuck, who was always one for a joke. " You were saved by the skin of a deer! "

And they all laughed. In fact, when the story got round, everybody laughed. Everybody, that is, except the Sheriff of Nottingham.

Series 549